DATE DUE

FEB 1 5			
FEB 2 9			
JAN 0 7			
GAYLORD			PRINTED IN U.S.A.

RL 4.5
PT 0.5

HOW CHIPMUNK GOT TINY FEET

NATIVE AMERICAN ANIMAL ORIGIN STORIES

Collected and Retold by Gerald Hausman

Illustrated by Ashley Wolff

HarperCollins*Publishers*

For Ricia
—G. H.

For Peri
—A. W.

Grateful acknowledgment is made to Navajo Curriculum Center, Phoenix, Arizona; Navajo Nights / Sunset Productions, Santa Fe, New Mexico; The Bureau of American Ethnology Reports; The Santa Fe Public Library; The Wheelwright Museum of the American Indian; and storytellers Bluejay DeGroat, Raymond Brown, and Ray Tsosie.

The illustrations in this book are linoleum block prints painted with watercolors.

How Chipmunk Got Tiny Feet
Native American Animal Origin Stories
Text copyright © 1995 by Gerald Hausman
Illustrations copyright © 1995 by Ashley Wolff
Printed in Mexico. All rights reserved.

Library of Congress Cataloging-in-Publication Data
Hausman, Gerald.
    How Chipmunk got tiny feet : Native American animal origin stories /
collected and retold by Gerald Hausman ; illustrated by Ashley Wolff.
        p.   cm.
    Contents: How Coyote got yellow eyes—How Bat learned to fly—
How Lizard got flat—How Hawk stopped the flood with his tail
feather—How Horse got fast—How Possum lost his tail—How
Chipmunk got tiny feet.
    ISBN 0-06-022906-3. — ISBN 0-06-022907-1 (lib. bdg.)
    1. Indians of North America—Legends.   2. Animals—Folklore.
[1. Indians of North America—Legends.   2. Animals—Folklore.]
I. Wolff, Ashley, ill.   II. Title.
E98.F6H525   1995   92-44186
398.24'5'08997—dc20   CIP
                                                                 AC

Typography by Elynn Cohen
1   2   3   4   5   6   7   8   9   10
❖
First Edition

TABLE OF CONTENTS

INTRODUCTION

In these seven origin tales, we learn how the animals came to be what they are today, and also the universal message they offer as Native American symbols. Most tribes hold the belief that animals are people who could once walk and talk like human beings. As creatures of origin, they are thought to be godlike, while their counterparts, the animals of today, are simply representatives of those ancient ones, their ancestors.

In every tribe, animals are thought of as people and are therefore called animal people. They have the same virtues, the same dilemmas, as humans; as these stories, we hope, demonstrate. In the words of a Santee Sioux storyteller: "We tell these stories not to entertain our children, but to educate them in the ways of the world. For this reason the moral of the story does not change—the way of the storyteller does. He may tell the story in different ways to make different points. Always the message is the same: Here is the world. . . . We must live in it together, not apart."

Gerald Hausman

HOW COYOTE GOT YELLOW EYES

Coyote learned the game of Throw-Away-Eyes from Magpie. He was walking along one day when he saw Magpie spin around in the sky and throw away his eyes. "That is a neat trick," Coyote said. "Could you teach me how to do it?"

"Coyotes cannot do that trick," Magpie replied smartly.

"I bet they can," Coyote bragged.

"Very well," said Magpie, "I will show you. But you must not get mad at me if you cannot catch up your eyes after you lose them."

So Magpie flew into the air, spun around four times, shook

his head from side to side, threw away his eyes, and caught them back in his head again. Coyote watched with eager attention. "I know how to do it," he said. And he ran in a straight line, spun around three times, shook his head up, down, and all around, and threw away his eyes; but he failed to catch them up. Two Blue Jays saw Coyote's eyes lying in the sand, and they took them up and flew away with them.

Now Coyote was stone blind. He called for Magpie, but Magpie was long gone.

"I cannot see," Coyote wailed. "Magpie, where are you?"

Ground Squirrel was nearby; he heard Coyote hollering. "Since I have never lost anything," he explained, "I don't think I could find anything. Sorry."

Badger came along just then and said, "I would not be much help to you; my claws would just get in the way."

Hummingbird whizzed by, saying, "With so many flowers to visit, I am much too busy to help you."

Then Coyote heard a kind voice, and he knew that it was Mother Earth. Who else was always helpful, and never cruel? Who but she would help someone who made a practice of never helping anyone?

"There, there, Coyote," she said. "I know of a person who can help you."

"No one helps me because no one likes me," Coyote cried.

"That is not true," Mother Earth replied in her kindly way. "I have asked Nuthatch to help you find your eyes."

No sooner had she said this than Nuthatch came around, saying, "Look, Coyote, I have brought you two new pine-gum eyes; I picked them off a piñon tree and made them for you myself."

"Oh, thank you, cousin Nuthatch," Coyote said.

Nuthatch flew down and put the two new eyes into Coyote's head. "I can see!" Coyote shouted, hopping up and down. Nuthatch, who had other things to do, flew away.

It was not very long before Coyote started remembering the animal people who had made up excuses so they would not have to help him. "I am going to steal Ground Squirrel's favorite nuts," he thought. "Then he will find out what it is like to lose something." After he had done this, he went to Badger's hole. "I will stop here a moment and fill Badger's house with dirt. Then he will have to put his claws to good use."

For the rest of the day Coyote did bad things to punish those animal people who had refused to help him. The last person he wanted to punish was Hummingbird. "Too busy to help cousin Coyote find his eyes," he said; and he spilled all the nectar out of Hummingbird's sacred red medicine bundle.

Now, it was so very hot that day that while Coyote was busy doing bad things, the sun shone down on his pine-gum eyes and started to melt them. "Oh no," he cried. "My eyes are melting!" Off he went, running madly, to cool them down. After a while they turned hard again, but not before the sticky gum had made two sooty streaks along the side of his face. These are the same markings that remind Coyote, even today, that his yellow eyes are made of sap.

Retold from a Navajo origin folktale told by storytellers
Ray Tsosie, Raymond Brown, and Bluejay DeGroat

HOW BAT LEARNED TO FLY

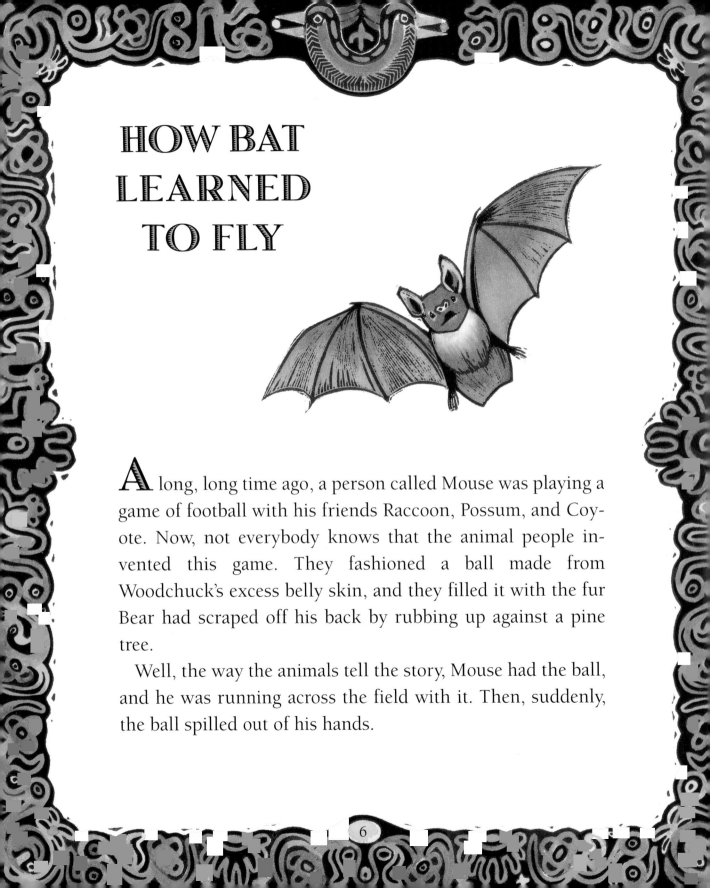

A long, long time ago, a person called Mouse was playing a game of football with his friends Raccoon, Possum, and Coyote. Now, not everybody knows that the animal people invented this game. They fashioned a ball made from Woodchuck's excess belly skin, and they filled it with the fur Bear had scraped off his back by rubbing up against a pine tree.

Well, the way the animals tell the story, Mouse had the ball, and he was running across the field with it. Then, suddenly, the ball spilled out of his hands.

Coyote, who was playing on his team, came up to him. "Why do you always drop the ball when you are running?" he asked Mouse.

"It's because he has such small hands," Raccoon said scoldingly.

Possum added, "Maybe he doesn't know how to hold the ball yet. . . ."

Mouse listened to his friends, who just wanted to be helpful; but the truth was, all of them had bigger hands than Mouse. They could hold the ball any way they wanted, and they wouldn't drop it, ever. But no matter how hard Mouse tried, the ball was too large for him to run with.

"Try it this way," Raccoon suggested. And he showed Mouse the way he liked to hold the ball, Raccoon style, under his big arm.

"Don't hold it like that," Possum broke in. "I always put it under my chin." And Possum showed Mouse how he could put the ball under his chin, which was as long as Alligator's.

Mouse went away and sat under a persimmon tree. How sorry he felt for himself! He would not play football with his friends anymore—he was just too ashamed.

Then Mouse heard a gentle voice. "Mouse, do not be sad. For you have something the other animal people do not have."

Mouse looked up, and he saw Mother Earth with her long hair and a green gown that looked like spring rain.

Mother Earth spoke with a voice of summer wind. "Every day," she said softly, "I have watched you play, and I know that one day you will be a fine player of football."

"But how?" Mouse asked. "I cannot even hold the ball."

"From now on when you play," Mother Earth answered, "jump up when you see the ball coming to you. Wrap yourself around it."

Mouse thought about this for a moment. "Well," he replied, "I am a good jumper!"

"Remember," she said. "Catch the ball with your whole body: Spread your arms when you jump, and jump as high as you can. . . ."

So Mouse thanked Mother Earth. When she went on her way, he remembered what she had said about catching the ball.

"Maybe," he mused, "just maybe, it will work."

Now the next time Mouse played a game of football, he leaped high into the air. The ball went into his soft belly fur, and Mouse wrapped his whole body around it. He went flying through the air. No one, not even Coyote, could catch him.

Raccoon and Possum were completely surprised. Where had Mouse learned such a great trick? When Coyote tried it himself, he fell flat on his face and made a fool of himself.

From that time on, whenever the ball came to Mouse, he leaped up, wrapped himself all around it—just the way Mother Earth said he should—and soared through the air. No one, not even Cardinal, could catch him.

After a while, Mouse became the best, the fastest, the smartest football player there ever was, and everyone said he was the champion of the game.

One day, so the animal people say, Mouse jumped up and flew right over the ball. They say he went so high in the sky, he never came down.

"I can actually fly!" Mouse laughed as he soared through air.

"Yes," Mother Earth told him. "You can fly, for you are no longer Mouse."

"Do I have a new name?"

"You are the one we shall now call Bat," Mother Earth answered.

And he has been called that name ever since that time.

Retold from a traditional Koasati Creek folktale

HOW LIZARD
GOT FLAT

They say Lizard was once a fat fellow who could not move very fast. When food came along, he hardly had to move to get it. You see, Lizard's food was mostly Ant. This was what made Lizard such a lazy fellow. Life was easy for him. He never worried—unlike other animal people—where his next meal was coming from. It just came walking along, right into his mouth.

Well, one day, a long time ago, Coyote was out hunting. He was walking in the hot sun, searching for something to eat. He saw Lizard, who was a very fancy dresser, all decked out in his best clothes, lying on a rock.

"Hmm," Coyote said to himself. "Here's a fat, lazy fellow who is too slow to know that I'm about to have him for lunch."

Smiling, Coyote trotted over to the rock.

"Nice day," he said slyly to Lizard.

"Yeah," Lizard said.

"Have you ever played the game called Rock-the-Rock?" Coyote asked.

"No," said Lizard. "I don't happen to like games—too much work."

"So what do you do all day?" Coyote asked, drooling.

"I lie here in the sun." Lizard yawned. "What else is there to do?"

"Well, you could play Rock-the-Rock," Coyote said, licking his whiskers. Then, quickly, before Lizard could protest, Coyote got behind the rock Lizard was lying on, and he gave it a little push. The rock was on a hill, so it started to rock back and forth; then it started to roll.

Coyote ran after it, but the rock—with Lizard holding on tight—rolled out of sight, around the bend.

"Lizard, where are youuu?" Coyote called out in a false-friendly voice.

This was all part of the game.

But there was no answer. Lizard, stuck to the rock, had rolled way down the canyon.

"Hmm," said Coyote. "Sometimes getting a quick bite to eat is more work than fun."

Just then he spied Stinkbug nosing along. To Coyote, who doesn't mind bad-smelling things—he smells awful himself—a fresh Stinkbug is worth more than a lost Lizard.

And so off he went, after an easier, if smellier, meal.

But now Lizard was trapped under that rock. He could not move because the rock was on top of him. He tried to wiggle his nose, but the rock pressed upon him, and he could hardly draw a breath.

The day wore on; the sun sank. Lizard kept trying to free himself from that rock. And after a time, he managed to get his nose out from under it. But the rest of him was still trapped.

Several days went by, and Lizard began to lose weight. He began to get skinny. Then he began to get flat. You would have thought—looking at him—that he was not Lizard but Snake.

And that was how he got free: pretending he hadn't any legs, and just slithering out from under the rock the way Snake did.

But when he saw himself in a pool of water, he was dreadfully unhappy. For his fancy suit of clothes had rubbed off on the rock, while the rock's drab-looking brown skin had rubbed off on him. And Lizard's body was so flat that if he had tried to stand up, he would have fallen over like a leaf.

"I'm not pretty and fat anymore," he cried miserably. "Why, if my arms fell off right now, I would be mistaken for Snake!"

Then a kind voice said, "Do not feel bad, Lizard. You may not be beautiful, but you will no longer be quite so lazy."

Lizard looked up and saw Mother Earth, dressed in an autumn robe of the softest brown.

"You see," she told him, "you are the same color as the desert rock you lie on."

Lizard smiled, because he realized that what Mother Earth said was true. Coyote was going to have a hard time tricking him now.

And ever since that time, Lizard has been proud to be thin as a leaf and rough skinned as a rock. For when he wants to hide, all he has to do is close his eyes . . . and disappear.

Adapted from a traditional Navajo folktale

HOW HAWK STOPPED THE FLOOD WITH HIS TAIL FEATHER

Now there was once a person named Water Monster, who was large and fat, and very oily. The animal people were much afraid of her because it was she who controlled all the water in the land.

Every morning when she woke, she said: "Give me some water!" And the animal people had to run to the river, fill up their water jars, and rush them back to Water Monster.

Well, one day the river went dry. Badger complained to Weasel about it. "Now we have to walk all the way to the lake to get Water Monster's drinking water."

Weasel agreed, "That one is never satisfied."

Badger groaned, "Soon there will not be any water left."

"Then what will be done?" Weasel wanted to know.

And the day came when the lake did go dry. The sun came up in the east and went down in the west, but it did not rain anymore. The sky was hot and there were no clouds. The animal people were fearful. Something terrible, they felt, was going to happen.

"Water Monster's to blame for this," Pine Marten said.

"What can we do?" Weasel persisted.

"I know," said Redbird. "We can send Wolf, the Big Wanderer, over the mountain to see if there is any water on the other side."

All agreed that this was a good plan. So Wolf was called and told what to do, and he went off with a smile on his face. However, Wolf did not come back.

"He moves like the rain," Redbird explained, "sometimes here, sometimes there. Hardly ever where you want it."

Weasel, who was always worried, added: "Maybe Water Monster drank him down."

"I do not think so," Little Hawk told them. "Your scout, Wolf, just got tired of looking, and he went away. He is selfish, that one."

"What do we do?" Weasel mumbled nervously.

None of the animal people seemed to know. So they sat in a circle and looked up at the sky. It was then that Mother Earth appeared in a garment of spotted clouds, with blue arrows of lightning on it.

"Do not fear," she told the animal people. "Someone among you has a special gift, and this gift will bring the water back."

"Who is this person?" questioned Redbird.

"He is the one with four black marks on his tail," Mother Earth replied. "Four marks for the four seasons of the year."

Right away, all the animal people looked at their tails.

Raccoon counted. "I have six marks."

"Too many," said Redbird.

"I have two," counted Skunk.

"Too few," said Redbird.

Bobcat said, "I have none."

"Too bad," said Redbird.

Then Little Hawk flew overhead. All the animal people looked up.

"Do you not see?" Mother Earth asked. "Little Hawk is the one who will set things right."

And so the animal people gave Little Hawk the honor of

being named the Scout of the Sky; for though he was not as large as Raven, nor as bold as Eagle, he was the only one with a four-marked tail.

Then he flew all over the earth, looking for something. After a while, he came upon what looked like a swamp that breathed; it was as tall as a mountain and it smelled quite foul.

"I will put an end to it," Little Hawk said to himself, and he shot an arrow into the side of it. That was the end of Water Monster. But then Little Hawk flew down to retrieve his arrow. As he pulled it out, a flood came out of Water Monster's belly. The water filled the whole valley.

Then the animal people had to climb to the top of the highest mountain to keep from being drowned.

"Little Hawk has caused this terrible flood," Redbird cried.

"Patience, children," Mother Earth said. "Put your faith in Little Hawk, and he will see you through this difficult time."

So the animal people promised to have faith in Little Hawk.

But Redbird said to him, "What can you do to make the flood go away?"

Little Hawk dropped out of the sky and plucked one of his four-marked tail feathers. "The flood," he said, "shall go no farther than this." He planted his tail feather on top of that

mountain, and his feather was his faith.

The flood rose to the fourth mark on that tail feather, and went no farther; then it began to recede. After this, the animal people praised Little Hawk. They said a good many things about him, all of them very fine. And Little Hawk took the feather out of the mountaintop and put it back in his tail. The flood was gone, the rivers and lakes were full of water; and Little Hawk, to this day, is still called the Scout of the Sky, in honor of his watchfulness.

Retold from a traditional Tsimshian folktale

HOW HORSE
GOT FAST

Horse was not always fast. He used to look at the sky and dream he was Eagle, racing across the blue. But whenever he picked up his feet, they were so heavy he could barely lift them. "You know," Raven said to him one spring day, "you were just not made right. Your weight is in your feet. No wonder you cannot run!"

And it was true. Horse was the slowest, most heavy-footed person around; still, his heart was just about the lightest. "One day," he told Raven, "I will fly like Eagle!"

Raven sat on a juniper branch chuckling. "You will never

do such a thing. You are just Horse, the Heavy-Footed One. Everyone knows that."

When he was alone, Horse said to himself: "Oh, but my feet are heavy! I wish someone would lighten them for me." And just then there came a voice upon the wind. Horse looked up and saw Mother Earth with her arms outspread. She wore a gown of blue winds about her shoulders; her hair was a white waterfall in the sun. All around her throat was a double rainbow necklace of pink, blue, gold and green.

"I have good words for you, Horse," she said. "You have a light heart but stone-heavy feet. We must keep the one and drop the other."

"How can we do this?" Horse wanted to know.

"Soon," she said, "you will help someone. After that, you will dance on the clouds."

Horse wanted to know more, but the voice of Mother Earth faded away in the wind and turned to the softest rain. The sun came out, the sky was clear; and Horse plodded along, as before, lifting each foot as if it were a mountain.

"Do not step on me," a tiny voice said.

"Who are you?" Horse asked, looking around. Then he saw a little crawling Caterpillar under one of his great shaggy feet.

"Do not worry, Caterpillar," Horse said. "I will not harm you."

However, Horse had to stand a long time on three legs before Little Caterpillar got out from under the shadow of his foot. The time wore on and on; Little Caterpillar moved slowly, slowly, slowly. First his front feet inched forward, then his back feet. This took such a long time that Horse thought he was going to fall over on his side from standing still so long. But at last, Little Caterpillar got out of his way.

"Now it is my turn to help you, Horse," he said.

"How could you possibly help me?" Horse asked.

"You do not see me as I really am," Little Caterpillar said, raising himself up to his full height.

"You are Little Caterpillar," said Horse.

"I am also known as Wind Dancer," cried Little Caterpillar.

Horse tried to think of Little Caterpillar dancing in the wind, but he could not do it. Little Caterpillar was just Little Caterpillar. "We," he said sadly, "are just what we are. You have many feet, all of them quite slow. I have four feet, all of them quite heavy. It comes to the same thing."

Little Caterpillar raised himself up a little higher. "Do you not know what season this is?" he asked.

Horse shook his head. "What difference does that make?" he asked.

"It is summer," Little Caterpillar laughed, "time to be . . ."

Horse watched as Little Caterpillar changed into a beautiful creature that danced on the wind.

"—Butterfly, The Wind Dancer."

Bright wings flashed, dazzling in their beauty.

"You have shown me kindness," Butterfly said to Horse. "Now I will do the same." Then Butterfly flew to the sacred mountain where flint was kept; and he flew back to Horse and put a magic flint in each of Horse's feet.

"I can dance," Horse shouted triumphantly. "I can dance upon a cloud!" And with that, he leaped into the air and soared up toward the sun.

Then a voice said, "Horse, you have brought much happiness into the world. From this time on, all horses will have feet as light as yours."

Horse could not contain his joy; he danced upon a cloud, tossing his mane in the wind.

Mother Earth watched him. She was wearing a butterfly shawl that fell from her shoulders like summer snow. "You belong to the Sun Father now," she said. "He will give you a sunbeam for a bridle when he rides across the sky."

From that day on all horses have loved to dance. And now you know why their tracks in the soft sand look like two wings: It is because of Little Caterpillar, who is also Butterfly, The Wind Dancer.

Adapted from a Navajo origin tale told by Bluejay DeGroat

HOW POSSUM LOST HIS TAIL

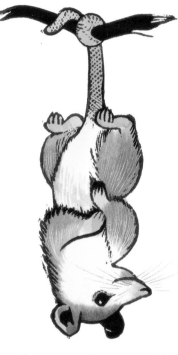

Skunk was feeling poorly, and it was not because he was ill. He was sick with jealousy. Every time he looked at Possum's big, silver, bushy tail, he thought of his own mean, bony tail, and it made him miserable.

Well, one morning, he saw Cricket hopping along, and he said: "Cousin Cricket, let us have a talk."

Cricket, a friendly fellow, hopped over.

"How are you getting along, my friend?" Cricket asked politely.

"The truth is, cousin, I am not well," Skunk confessed.

Cricket said, "What is the matter?"

Skunk hung his head dejectedly. "The trouble is . . ."

He paused, wondering how to say it.

"Yes?" Cricket said.

"To put it bluntly," Skunk admitted, "you see, Cricket, I have this awful tail that I am not the least bit proud of."

Cricket looked at Skunk's unbecoming tail. And, well, to be perfectly honest, which he almost always was, he had to agree with his friend's opinion.

"The way of the world," Skunk mournfully stated, "is that the person who has no need of a fine tail is usually the owner of the best one."

"Are you thinking of someone in particular?" Cricket wondered.

"Why, Possum, of course!" Skunk said.

"So true," Cricket commented, "now that you mention it. Possum is a shabby person, who cares nothing for the keeping of his tail. I do not think he knows that he has one."

"So now do you know why I am feeling low?"

"I do," replied Cricket. "But is there nothing that can be done about it?"

"Have you any thoughts, Cricket?"

Cricket thought a moment. Then he answered, "Yes, there

is something, I think, that might be done." And Cricket whispered into Skunk's ear.

That night, while Possum was asleep, Cricket crept into his cave, nibbled his tail off, and brought it directly to Skunk.

Skunk admired Possum's tail greatly. "Why, it is less a tail than a silver cloud!" he said, stroking it with pleasure.

"And it is all yours," Cricket said. "You know, just as quickly as I took it off Possum, I can put it on you."

"Put it on now," begged Skunk.

And Cricket stitched Possum's tail on Skunk.

The next morning, while Skunk was going around showing off his new tail, Possum was telling his friend Tree Squirrel of his bad luck. "This was the night I was going to visit Silver Fox to ask if she would be my wife."

Tree Squirrel was wise in the ways of the world, and he liked giving his friend Possum sound advice. "Do not be sad about this small thing," he mused. "You still have the best coat in the land. Go to Silver Fox with your coat nice and clean, and it will be just fine."

Possum's face brightened. He thanked Tree Squirrel and began cleaning his coat down by the river. That evening everything went as planned. Possum showed up in his fine white coat. He puffed out his chest and sat on his tailbone, so Silver

Fox would not see it. Silver Fox was so taken by his confidence, she never noticed that anything was amiss.

They sat under a persimmon tree with big, golden fruits hanging from its limbs. "Would you care for a fruit?" Possum asked. When she said yes, he stood up and, baring the wrong side of him, gave Silver Fox a good look at his missing tail.

Now she herself had a such a fine tail that the sight of Possum's stub made her feel most uncomfortable.

"What would people say if they saw me hanging around with someone who has a sawed-off rat tail?" she asked complainingly.

Well, poor Possum went home that night with his head hanging and his chin dragging. On the way to his cave, he met Skunk and Cricket.

"Now there's a tail I wish was mine," Possum said as he noticed Skunk's new tail.

Possum did not seem to realize that it had once belonged to him.

"You could have one just as grand." Skunk smiled falsely.

"Do you think so?"

"Look, there's a beautiful tail hanging up in that nut tree," Skunk lied.

"Someone must have left it there for you," Cricket added.

Possum let out a wild cry and scrambled up the nut tree.

Then Mother Earth appeared in front of Skunk and Cricket. She was taller than the nut tree, and her flowing hair was like the long moss that breathes in the wind. She wore moccasins of gold-brown and a necklace of pink shell.

"You should be ashamed of yourself, Skunk, tricking your cousin like that," Mother Earth said. "And you, Cricket, what sneaky tricks have you been playing?"

Cricket felt so ashamed he could hardly speak. He just sat there trembling, making a peeping sound.

"That is the way you will talk from this time on," Mother Earth said to him.

And he always has.

Skunk could do nothing but hide his face with his tail, and Mother Earth said: "From this day forward, you will always be bashful for what you have done."

And he always has been.

For his part, Possum never got over all the tricks that were played on him, which is why his mouth hangs open all the time, even to this day.

But let us not forget where Possum was—still up in that nut tree. He was not much of a climber, and when he tried to go up, he slipped down. Suddenly, he fell.

Mother Earth called to him: "Possum, use your tail!"

And that funny, bony rat tail that Silver Fox had made fun of wrapped itself around a nut-tree branch and broke Possum's fall.

"Come down," Skunk begged. "We want to be your friends."

"We're sorry we played tricks on you," Cricket chirped.

However, Possum never would come down from that tree; he liked where he was, hanging by his tail, upside down. And, to tell the truth, he has been that way ever since.

Retold from a traditional Koasati Creek folktale

HOW CHIPMUNK GOT TINY FEET

Once Chipmunk worked all day long as Gila Monster's watchman. His job was to make sure no one came around to steal anything out of Gila Monster's garden. But although Chipmunk was a pretty good watchman most of the time, some of the time he liked to fill his own pouches with Gila Monster's best corn kernels. He liked Gila Monster's corn very much, and every now and then he took some home with him.

One day Gila Monster noticed that his corn stalks were looking kind of thin. He did not know that Chipmunk had many cousins of the Mountain Squirrel clan; and that all of them had been visiting him. Each one had been given a gift of cornmeal. "This is my present to you, from Gila Monster's sacred garden," Chipmunk said to each of his cousins, when he presented them with his gift.

"Are you certain we may take this?" they asked. They were, and rightly so, afraid of Gila Monster. He was known to be secretive and not very friendly, and he had many powers. They had also heard stories about his temper. But Chipmunk assured his cousins they could have the cornmeal; to prove it, he gave them extra bags to take home.

Now, for some time, Gila Monster had suspected that Chipmunk was stealing from his garden. "Tell me," he said gruffly to Messenger Fly, "if you ever see Chipmunk making off with any of my corn plants."

One day Messenger Fly showed up at Gila Monster's cave. "You will be angry when you hear what I have seen," he said.

"Do not play games with me," Gila Monster said, impatiently. "Just say what you have to say."

Messenger Fly told of Chipmunk's visitors, the Mountain Squirrels. "He steals much, and he gives it to all his relations."

"Summon him, then," Gila Monster roared.

Messenger Fly delivered the message promptly. "You had

better come now," Messenger Fly warned. "Gila Monster thinks you are a thief." But Chipmunk was feeling lazy that day, and he did not wish to be bothered. The next day he was warned again; and the day after that; and the day after that. When four days had gone by, Gila Monster himself came to Chipmunk's dwelling.

He rapped four times on Chipmunk's door with an old root cane that he carried. "Come outside, Chipmunk," he growled. "I would have a word with you."

Chipmunk was warm and cozy in his bedroll of sheep fur. "I cannot come to the door," he called. "I am too snug in bed."

So Gila Monster banged four more times on Chipmunk's door. The door blew open and a gust of wind struck Chipmunk across the face. Gila Monster walked in; his front feet, holding the cane unsteadily, were shaking with rage. "You have broken my command," he rasped, red and black in the face. "Now, little thief, what have you to say for yourself?"

"Let me sleep," Chipmunk said stuffily. "I was up late with my Mountain Squirrel cousins."

"I will teach you to steal my corn kernels," Gila Monster hissed with blast of foul breath. He blew four times on his root cane, and Chipmunk shrank down to the size of an ant.

He was so small, you could hardly see him. Then Gila Monster went back to his cave and thought no more about it.

For his part, Chipmunk was sorry for what he had done. Yet he was even more sorry for the state in which he found himself. His lodge was too large for him; he now lived inside a nutshell that he had once cast aside. He was lonely and quite miserable.

"Whatever will I do?" he cried. "No one even knows that I am here. My cousins never come to visit anymore. I am so little that I cannot find any clothes to wear." He had wrapped himself in a leaf, but it was still too big for him.

"Little Chipmunk, I see where you are," a warm, loving voice said to him one day. It was, of course, Mother Earth, who now appeared the same size as Chipmunk.

"You are small," he said, and somehow he managed to smile.

"I am whatever size I wish to be, Chipmunk," she said tenderly. Her hair was like the red roots that reach down into the rose-colored soil; her skin was dove gray like the color of blue corn.

"It is cold to be so small," Chipmunk chattered.

"That is because you are so far from the sun," she explained.

"What can I do?" he asked. "You know that I will never steal again."

"You must go to Gila Monster and tell him," Mother Earth said. "Maybe then he will free you from his magic spell."

So Chipmunk journeyed to Gila Monster's cave. Because he was so small, it took him a long time. He had many adventures along the way, but finally he arrived at the great lizard's doorway. "Do not step on me, Gila Monster," he hollered. "It is I, your poor watchman, Chipmunk."

Gila Monster opened his door and squinted his fiery eye. "Ah, I see you there," he said laughing. "A bit of nothing that has a voice."

"Please set me free from your spell," Chipmunk pleaded.

"What gift have you brought for me?" the big lizard wanted to know.

"I brought a grain of golden pollen," Chipmunk answered respectfully.

Gila Monster blinked his molten eye. After a time, he replied: "It is good, little one. You have come to own up to what you did, and you have brought me a ceremonial gift."

Then he banged his root cane four times, and the earth shook. Chipmunk held on to a pebble to keep from being knocked down. After this, Gila Monster took out his

medicine bundle and blew some smoke at the sun, and at the earth, and in the four directions. Then he blew a little of it on Chipmunk, who right away began to grow back into himself. He grew and grew.

Soon he was just the way he had always been before Gila Monster had shrunk him. But now he tottered and fell: His feet would not hold him up. "Oh, my feet," he wailed. "They are so small!"

"And they shall remain so," Gila Monster proclaimed, "so that you will remember your sacred trust: that you must never steal again, from anyone."

"I will never steal again, from anyone," Chipmunk vowed.

"I believe you," Gila Monster said. "That is why I have restored you." And he went back into his cave.

Chipmunk, his wobbly little feet taking him home, was glad to be who he was. He did not care about his feet being little, just so the rest of him was the right size. And he never stole a corn kernel ever again from Gila Monster's garden. But to this day, all chipmunks have tiny feet.

Retold from a traditional Navajo folktale